EGMONT

We bring stories to life

First published in Great Britain in 2020 by Egmont Books UK Ltd.,
2 Minster Court, 10th floor, London EC3R 7BB
www.egmontbooks.co.uk

Written and edited by Katrina Pallant
Designed by Jeannette OToole for Ruby Shoes Limited

Parental guidance is advised for all craft and colouring activities.
Always ask an adult to help when using glue, paint and scissors.
Wear protective clothing and cover surfaces to avoid staining.

Stay safe online. Egmont is not responsible for content hosted
by third parties.

Egmont takes its responsibility to the planet and its inhabitants
very seriously. We aim to use papers from well-managed
forests run by responsible suppliers.

ISBN 978 1 4052 9961 9
71271/003
Printed in Italy

This
Disney Christmas Annual 2021
belongs to

Drumcondra Branch Te.

....

~~SEP 2020~~   May 2021

....

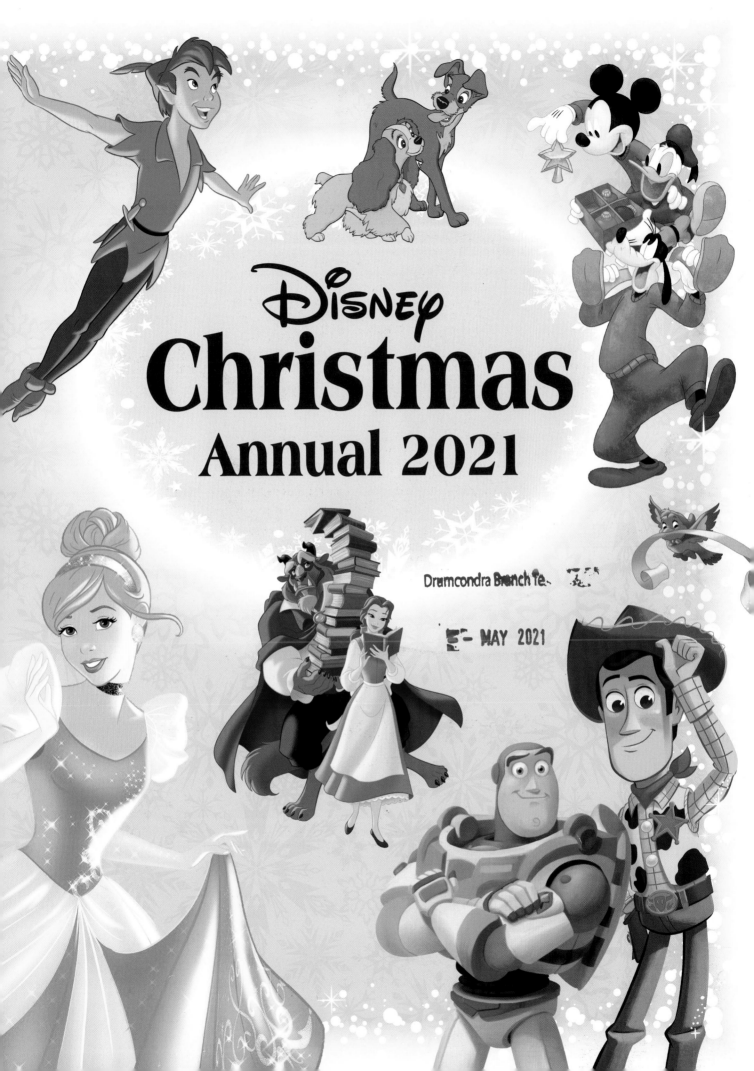

Disney
Christmas
Annual 2021

Contents

Disney Cinderella

Disney 101 DALMATIANS

Disney Peter Pan

Disney Lady and the TRAMP

A Toy Christmas

Andy was playing in his room with his favourite toys when his mum came in and sat on his bed.

"Andy, I have a surprise for you," she said. "This year for your Christmas present ... we're going to the Grand Canyon!"

"Hooray!" Andy cheered. "Can I take Buzz and Woody?"

"Leave them here," his mother replied. "You'll be too busy to play."

As soon as Andy and his mum left the room, the toys came to life. Most of the toys were excited that Andy was getting a trip instead of any new toys. But Woody realised it also meant they would be spending Christmas without Andy!

"We'll just make it a toy Christmas!"
said Buzz, trying to cheer up his friend.
"Buzz is right, we'll have a great Christmas,"
Woody said. But he didn't believe it.
Without the kid that loved them,
it wouldn't be much fun at all.

After Andy and his family left on their trip, the toys started getting ready for Christmas.

Jessie showed Woody a red bandana that was the perfect present for Bullseye.

Wheezy invited Woody to sing carols, but nothing was getting Woody in the Christmas spirit. It all just reminded him how sad he'd be without Andy.

"Hey, Woody, want to help us decorate?" Slinky Dog asked.

Two Aliens bounced super-high and draped a string of red and green buttons along the edge of the bookcase. The army commander and his troops hung sparkly silver jacks that looked like snowflakes across the room.

In the corner was a Christmas tree made entirely of cotton balls with red and green hair ribbons wrapped around it. Underneath there were presents wrapped in shiny paper and topped with colourful bows.

Woody smiled a little bit, but it still didn't feel the same without Andy.

"Come on, Woody", said Buzz. "I have some Christmas magic to show you."
The space ranger pressed the laser button on his right arm over and over again
sending a beam of red light onto the wall. The light pulsed around the room making
a show of dancing snowflakes, sugarplums and toys.
"Wow, Buzz!" cried Woody. "That's really great!"
Rex rode in with RC wearing a white cotton beard
and a red sock hat. "Ho, ho, rrrroooarr!"
He went to the tree and started handing out presents.
Woody looked at his friends. Buzz was right. Christmas
was about spending time with the toys you loved!
"Merry Christmas, everyone!"

Paper Chains

Woody and the gang love Christmas, especially all the festive decorations. Make these Toy Story paper chains with an adult and decorate your room!

Instructions

Cut out the paper strips – make some more with your own paper and pens.

Take one strip and curl it around in a circle and glue the two ends together.

Feed your next strip through the middle of the first, curl round and glue the two ends together.

Repeat until you have linked all the strips and hang your finished festive paper chain.

Odd One Out

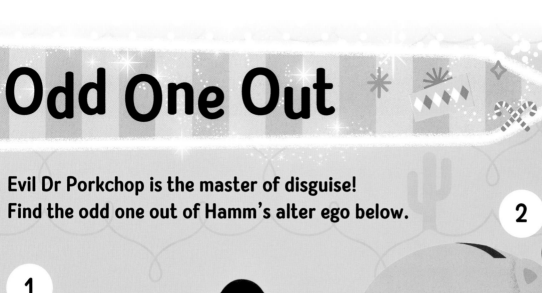

Evil Dr Porkchop is the master of disguise!
Find the odd one out of Hamm's alter ego below.

1

2

4

3

Meet the Gang!

Woody

is a cowboy sheriff with a pull-string and he is Andy's favourite toy! He is the leader of the group and always helps the other toys. He can sometimes get a bit jealous, but is an extremely loyal friend. Woody believes toys should do anything for their kid!

Buzz Lightyear

is a space ranger from the Intergalactic Alliance with a laser pointer and pop-out wings. He is fearless, loves adventure and often helps his friends out of trouble with his heroic actions. Though they get off to a tricky start, Buzz and Woody are best friends.

Andy Davis

is the owner of the toys. He loves Woody and would not leave home without him throughout his childhood. He has a brilliant imagination and pretends his toys are on many adventures including having Woody and Buzz rescue Bo Peep from the evil Dr Porkchop!

Rex

is a nervous Tyrannosaurus rex living in Andy's room. He looks like the most fearsome toy in the box, but really he is lovable and only has a small roar. He is always worried that he will be replaced or left behind, but the other toys are able to reassure him.

Jessie

is a yodelling cowgirl who was once a member of Woody's Roundup Gang. She is very friendly and kind. She hates being cooped up in storage, and is always ready for an adventure with her kid. When she joins Andy's room, she finds true friends.

The Little Green Men

are squeezy toy aliens hailing from Pizza Planet. They worship the claw in the toy-grabbing machine and function using a hive-mind. The Potato Heads adopt them when they come to Andy's room and the LGM are very loyal. They even save the day when the toys are almost incinerated.

17

Let's Decorate!

Jessie and Bullseye are getting ready for Christmas by decorating the tree.

Best Friends

Woody and Buzz can't wait to exchange presents!

Present Problems

Listen to the story about Belle. When you see a picture, join in and say the word!

 Belle Mrs Potts present book

 Beast Cogsworth Lumiere presents

It was the week before Christmas, and had nearly finished wrapping all the for her new friends in the castle. But she couldn't decide what to give the .

 went to the kitchen to ask what she thought. "Well, dear, I think he might like a new brush!" was not convinced.

Next, went to speak to . He wasn't much help either. "I think the would like the repairs to the stable to be finished."

Finally, asked for his advice.

"You should paint him a grand portrait!"

he said. But was not very good at painting.

 was discouraged so she went to the library.

As she made her way around the shelves, she smiled.

"I know the perfect for the !"

On Christmas morning, was excited to give the

 his gift. He unwrapped it to reveal – a !

"It's my favourite!" the said. "Will you read it to me?"

he asked. The two settled down in front of a cosy fire

to read the new . "That was the best Christmas

 I ever received," said the .

Tangled Lines

Now you've read the story, see if you can help Belle find the Beast the perfect present. Which line will take Belle to the book?

a

b

c

Design your Own Stockings

Cogsworth is decorating the house for Christmas, but the stockings are looking a bit plain. Get your pencils and brighten up the stockings with patterns and colour.

Puzzle Pieces

Belle and the Beast are having a snow fight.
Find the missing piece of this picture below.

1

2

3

ANSWER: Piece 3 is the missing piece.

Counting

Christmas is in full swing at the castle. Count how many festive items are on this page and colour in the right number for each item below.

How many  1 2 3

How many  1 2 3

How many  1 2 3

Christmas Tracing

Trace the following festive words and match them with the pictures.

gift

star

tree

Shadow Match

Match up all of Belle's castle friends with their shadows.

a

b

c

d

1

2

3

4

Minnie Saves Christmas!

Mickey, Minnie and their friends had been working hard preparing for Christmas – and it was only one day away!

Donald looked up at the clock. "Aw, phooey! Christmas Eve is the longest day ever!"

Mickey smiled. "Don't worry, Donald. Christmas will be here before you know it!"

Just then, a timer rang. Minnie jumped up.

"My cookies are ready! Who wants one?" Just as she took the cookies out of the oven, there was a loud crash in the other room!

Goofy dove under the table. "Gawrsh! What was that?"

Minnie looked towards the living room. "It sounded like it came from the fireplace."

Donald looked excited. "Maybe it's Santa Claus!"

Everyone raced to the fireplace. But it wasn't Santa Claus ...
It was Mrs Claus! "Merry Christmas, everyone!"
Minnie was surprised. "Why, Mrs Claus, what brings you here?"

Mrs Claus looked at her friends. "Oh, I need your help! Santa accidentally shrunk his mittens and his big red bag when he ran them through the wash. And now I'm afraid he won't be able to deliver presents tonight!"

Minnie thought for a moment and then made a dash for the kitchen. "I know just what we need!"

Minutes later, Minnie returned with an armful of things. "Santa could use this big red tablecloth for a bag!"

Mrs Claus clapped her hands. "It's perfect, Minnie!"

"And we can tie it shut with this ribbon from my ribbon collection!"

Mickey shrugged. "But what about Santa's shrunken mittens?"

Minnie held up her Christmas oven mitts. "Ta-da!"

Mrs Claus beamed. "Oh, thank you, Minnie! You saved Christmas!"

Minnie giggled. "It was my pleasure!"

"Well, I'd better hurry back to the North Pole. Who wants to come with me?"

Everyone cheered as they climbed into the sleigh with Mrs Claus and took off into the sky.

Santa was waiting for them when they arrived at the North Pole. "Thank goodness you're back just in the nick of time!"

Minnie handed him his new bag and his extra-warm mittens.

Just then, Pluto started barking. He wanted to help, too!

Minnie gave Pluto a hug. "With a little of Santa's magic, I'm sure you can help pull the sleigh!"

She used the rest of her ribbon to make a special harness for Pluto – with an extra-special bow, of course!

Mrs Claus, Minnie and the rest of the gang waved as the reindeer – and Pluto – pulled Santa's sleigh up, up, up into the night sky. It was going to be the best Christmas ever!

Questions

Now you have read this festive Mickey story, see if you can answer the following questions.

1 Who made Christmas cookies?

    a   **Minnie**

    b   **Mickey**

    c   **Goofy**

2 Who came through the fireplace?

    a   **Easter bunny**

    b   **Mrs Claus**

    c   **Tooth fairy**

3 What got shrunk in the wash?

    a   **Santa's sleigh**

    b   **Santa's reindeer**

    c   **Santa's big red bag**

4 What does Minnie suggest Santa uses for his bag?

    a   **A coat**

    b   **A tablecloth**

    c   **A tent**

5 What does Minnie suggest Santa uses instead of his mittens?

    a   **Oven gloves**

    b   **Socks**

    c   **Tinsel**

6 Who gets to join the reindeer at the front of Santa's sleigh?

    a   **Donald**

    b   **Goofy**

    c   **Pluto**

ANSWER: 1. a. 2. b. 3. c. 4. b. 5. a. 6. c.

Special Delivery

Minnie helps to post the Christmas letters.

Carol Colouring

Mickey and Minnie are singing some festive songs.

Holiday Hunt

Help Mickey through the maze counting how many presents he collects for his friends along the way.

START

FINISH

Mickey collects **1 2 3 4 5** presents.

Circle the right number.

A Merry Christmas for Mice

Listen to the story about Cinderella. When you see a picture, join in and say the word!

Cinderella stepsisters stepmother presents

Jaq Gus present tiara

It was Christmas Eve and was feeling sad. Her and had gone away for the holidays and the empty house reminded her of celebrating with her father.

They had loved decorating and wrapping together.

 was worried. But he knew he could help. He called all his bird and mice friends to begin gathering holly, pine cones and mistletoe. found a small tree and her dog Bruno hauled it home on a sled. helped decorate it with colourful strands of fruit.

 started to wonder about Christmas dinner.

"Oh dear," said , "you must be very hungry."

She made a warm apple pie and served it to her friends

by a warm fire. "Thank you for sharing my Christmas,"

said .

"Waitee, waitee, Cinderelly!" said ."Gotta open

giftee." He pulled out a from behind his back.

 opened it revealing a 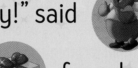 made out of

ribbons. and had made it for her and

decorated it with sparkly beads. When put the

 on they cheered! She looked at her good friends

and knew it was a merry Christmas after all.

Lost Property

Cinderella famously lost something on her escape from the ball. Join the dots to return her property to her.

16

15

17

14

18

13

8

19

1

12 9 7

2

20

3

6

11 10 5

4

Odd Mouse Out

Gus is Cinderella's loyal friend.
Which image of this lovable
mouse is the odd one out?

1

2

3

4

5

ANSWER: Picture 4.

41

Count and Colour

Cinderella has left her shoes all over the castle. Count the shoes then colour them in!

ANSWER: There are 6 shoes.

Mouse Maze

Help the mice sneak past Lucifer the cat without getting caught!

START

FINISH

Spot the Difference

Cinderella is ticking off her Christmas checklist. Can you find four differences between these two pictures?

ANSWER: Chair has changed colour, bird has appeared, cotton reel has appeared and feather pen is missing

The Puppies' First Christmas

One winter evening, Roger and Nanny hauled a huge tree into the parlour. The parlour floor was covered in pine needles, boxes of ornaments, tinsel and strings of lights. The puppies looked on as their human pets began acting very strangely. When the tree was finished, the lights and shiny ornaments cast a magical glow about the room.

That night, when Pongo and Perdita tucked the puppies into their basket, they told them all about Christmas.

"On Christmas Eve people put presents under the tree to show their love," Perdita said, "Christmas is about giving."
"I wonder if we will get any presents," said Rolly.
"I hope someone loves us," said Pepper.
"You are all loved whether or not there are presents under the tree," Perdita said. "Now time for bed. Tomorrow is a big day."

On Christmas morning, the puppies crept into the parlour. Sure enough, there were piles of brightly wrapped presents under the tree. The puppies dove in and tossed the packages around and ripped and tore at the coloured paper. When Roger and Anita came in the puppies hid.

Anita started to laugh. Roger chuckled, too, and said, "Looks like we had some help opening our gifts." Then, with a twinkle in his eye, he called, "Here, pups!" One by one, the puppies crept from their hiding spots. They gathered around the tree as Roger pulled out more packages. The puppies tore into the bright wrappings and the tangled ribbons.

Anita brought out a large basket. She handed each puppy a squeaky toy. "We like Christmas!" Pepper said. "But remember what we told you about Christmas?" Perdita asked. "It's a time for giving." "It's also about forgiving," Pongo said. "You were lucky that Roger and Anita weren't upset you unwrapped their presents." The puppies' heads drooped a little.

"We are loved," Penny said. She smiled. "You are all, each and every one of you, loved," Perdita assured her children. "And that's what Christmas is really all about," Pongo said as the puppies drifted off to sleep.

Questions

Now you have read this festive 101 Dalmatians story, see if you can answer the following questions.

What were Roger and Nanny doing that confused the puppies?

1
- a **Decorating the Christmas tree**
- b **Baking a cake**
- c **Dancing**

What did Pongo and Perdita say Christmas was about?

2
- a **Eating**
- b **Watching TV**
- c **Giving**

What did the puppies do when they woke up on Christmas morning?

3
- a **Open the wrong presents**
- b **Eat their lunch**
- c **Stay in bed**

What did Anita give the puppies for Christmas?

4
- a **Sweets**
- b **Squeaky toys**
- c **A book**

Which puppy said they liked Christmas?

5
- a **Patch**
- b **Lucky**
- c **Pepper**

ANSWER: 1-a, 2-c, 3-a, 4-b, 5-c.

Dalmatian Doodles

The Dalmatian puppies all have different coats.
Design your own pattern and colour it in. It doesn't
have to be black and white!

Puppy Pairs

The playful Dalmatians have got all mixed up.
Match up the puppies.

1

2

3

4

5

a

b

c

d

e

Christmas in Never Land

Listen to the story about Peter Pan. When you see a picture, join in and say the word!

 Peter Pan   Wendy   Lost Boys   tree   Tiger Lily   Tinker Bell

 sighed as she looked around the ' hideout. "It's almost Christmas back home. I wish we weren't missing it."

"What's a Christmas?" asked. "Christmas is a time to show people how much you care for them," said. "And there's always a beautiful covered with lights."

 had an idea. He sent to collect seashells and then gathered the together. "We're going to surprise and have Christmas here in Never Land!" he said. and the 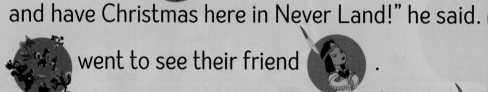 went to see their friend .

"We need presents for Christmas," told . "I know just the thing," replied. While helped make a beaded necklace for 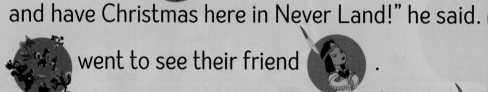 , her father taught the how to make arrowheads.

54

Next, (Peter Pan) and the (Lost Boys) scouted the forest for the perfect Christmas (tree) . They decorated it with the arrowheads and flowers but something was missing. "The lights!" exclaimed (Peter Pan) . "There's got to be a way to light the (tree) !" (Tinker Bell) put her hands on her hips and jingled at him. "Not now, (Tinker Bell) ," (Peter Pan) said.

(Peter Pan) came up with plan after plan to light the (tree) , but none worked. He tried to borrow some glowing fish from Mermaid Lagoon, but they couldn't live out of water. He tried to use fireflies but they kept flying away. "It's no use," (Peter Pan) said. "Without lights, what's the point in a (tree) ? Christmas is ruined." (Tinker Bell) marched up to (Peter Pan) and jingled as loud as she could. "Oh!" he realised. "You can make the (tree) light up! Why didn't you say so before?"

When (Wendy) returned, she found the hideout filled with light. The Christmas (tree) glowed with pixie dust. She gasped as (Peter Pan) and the (Lost Boys) burst out of their hiding places shouting "Merry Christmas!" (Wendy) smiled. Christmas had come to Never Land.

Lost Letters

Part of our flying hero's name is missing. Trace the letters to complete his name.

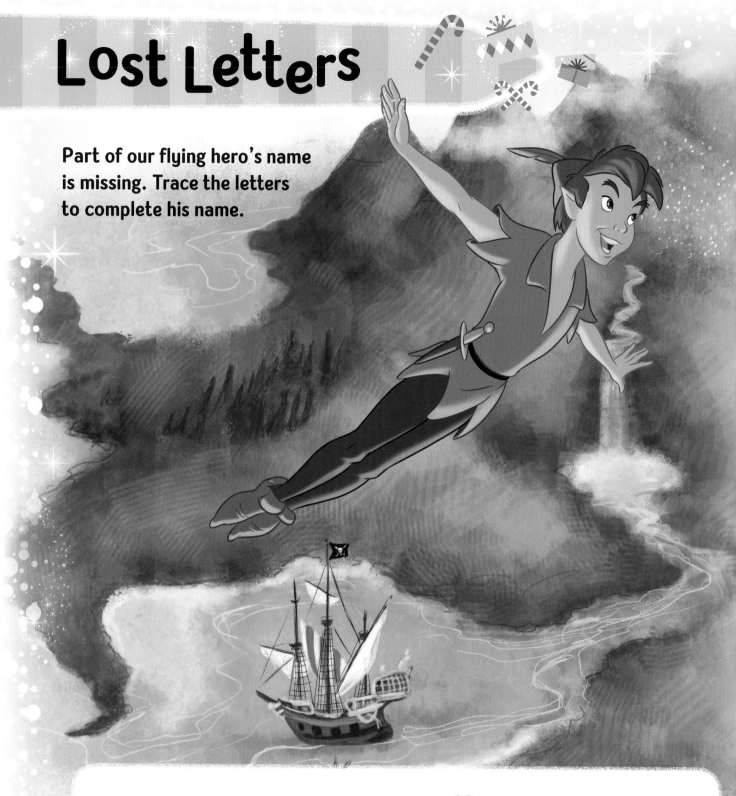

Peter Pan

Never Land Nonsense

Michael has been caught by Hook. Help Peter find him by travelling through the maze.

START

FINISH

Spot the Difference

The Lost Boys are sad it's not Christmas yet! Can you find the four differences between these two pictures?

ANSWER: Bowl is missing, Michael's outfit has changed colour, Lost Boy's ear is missing and John's umbrella has appeared.

Pan Puzzle

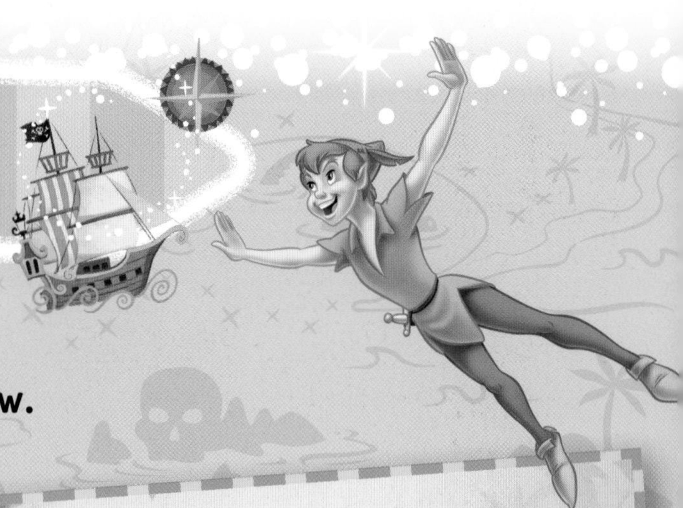

The Lost Boys are off on an adventure.
Find the missing piece of this picture below.

1

2

3

ANSWER: Shape 2 is the missing piece.

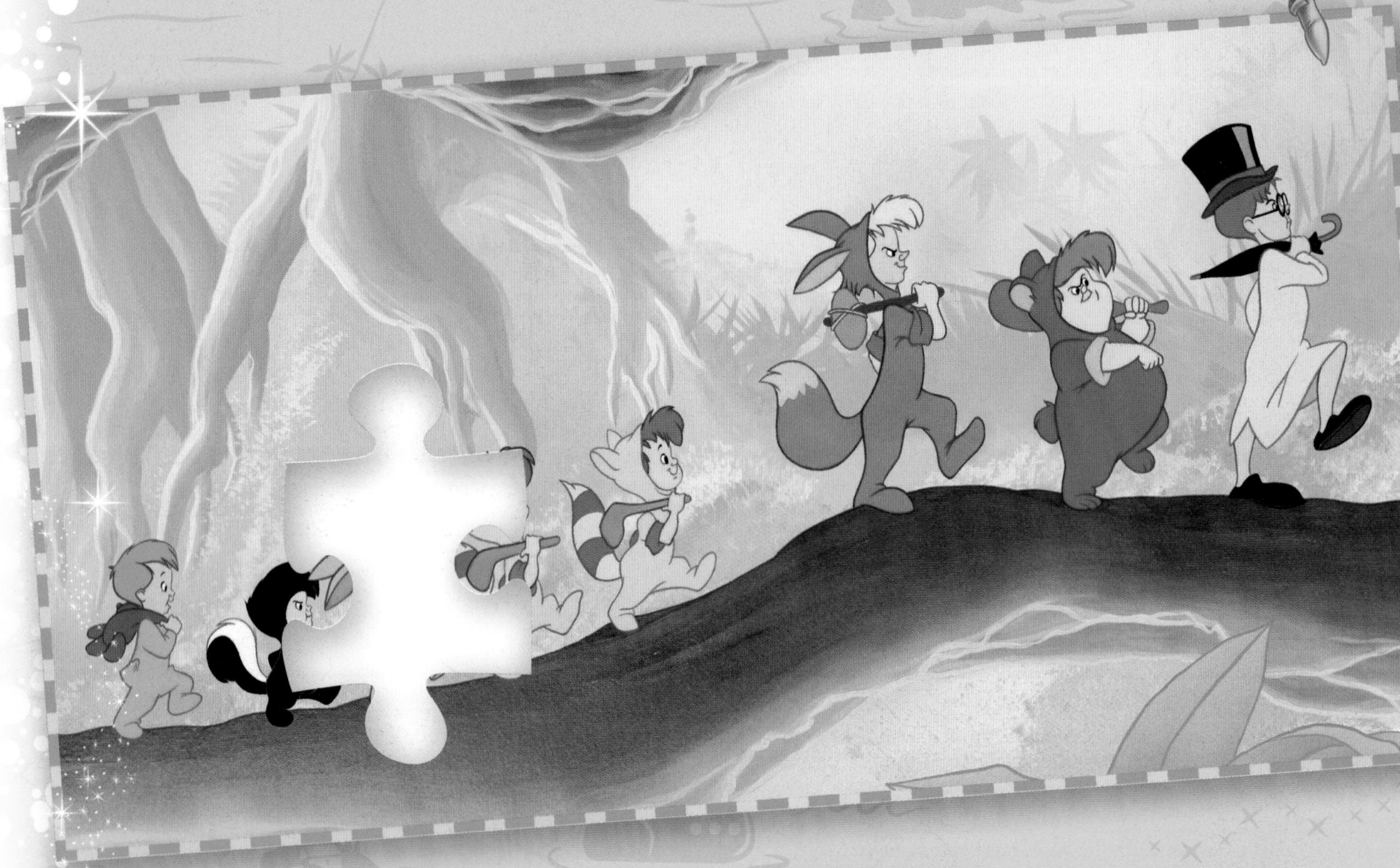

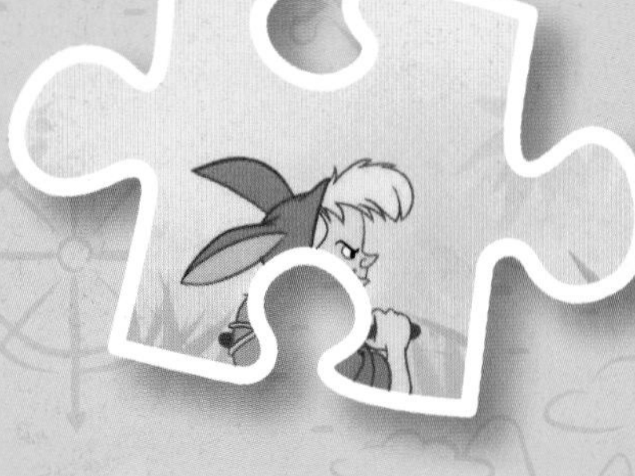

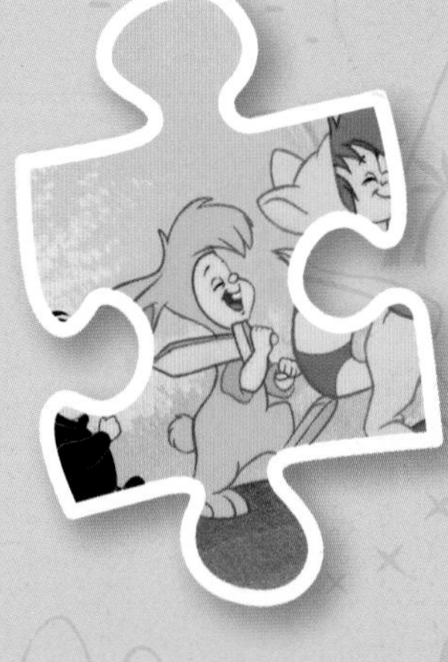

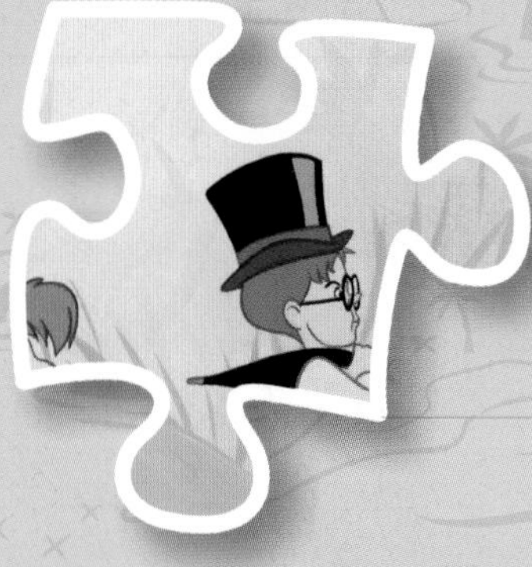

Shadow Match

Everyone on Never Land has lost their shadows.
Match the characters to their shadows.

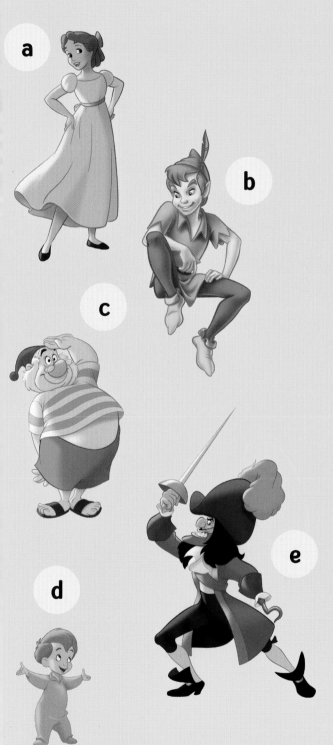

a

b

c

d

e

1

2

3

4

5

Lady's Christmas Surprise

It was the week before Christmas. Tramp and the puppies gathered beneath Jim and Darling's brightly decorated tree. The puppies were very excited. Christmas was their favourite holiday. The best part was the presents.

"Do any of you kids know what your mother would like for Christmas?" Tramp asked.

"We need to give her something special," said Colette, "to show we love her."

Tramp took the kids into town to look for the perfect present. The village bustled with shoppers. The dogs rambled up and down the avenue, looking in all the shop windows. They saw sweaters, cushions, brush and comb sets, bowls and collars. But Tramp knew that none of these things was the perfect gift for Lady. He wanted to find her something that she would enjoy and that no other dog would have.

As they crossed the road, Tramp noticed something sparkling in the snow. "Holy hambones!" he cried. It was a gold and diamond necklace! Tramp smiled and then scooped up the necklace with his mouth. They'd found the perfect gift. He knew it would look beautiful on Lady.

Suddenly, Tramp dropped the necklace into the snow. It sparkled in the icy crystals. He frowned.

"What's the matter?" Scamp asked.

"This isn't right," Tramp muttered. Then he looked at his children. "Sorry, kids, but we have to return the necklace. It's not ours to take."

With the puppies following, Tramp bounded down the block to the police station.

Tramp trotted up to the front desk, the puppies following behind. He dropped the necklace in front of the policeman in charge.

"What's this?" the officer said as he looked at the dog and then back to the necklace on the desk. Tramp panted and wagged his tail.

Yip! Yip!

"You found it?" the officer asked.

Tramp nodded.

"Good dog!" he exclaimed.

At that moment, a woman rushed into the station. "Help!" she cried.

"My necklace is gone!"

The policeman smiled at the woman. He pointed to Tramp. "This dog found it on the street and brought it here."

The woman gasped and scratched Tramp behind his ear. "How can I repay you?"

Woof! Tramp looked at the necklace. "A new collar," she said. "That's it!" She took Tramp to the shop next door. Tramp picked up a gold collar with green stones that looked just like the woman's necklace.

On Christmas morning Lady tore open the gift. "You shouldn't have!" she said. Her eyes sparkled like the green stones. "What a wonderful Christmas surprise! But I love my family even more." She nuzzled Tramp and each of the puppies.
"Merry Christmas, Mother," said the puppies.
And it was a very merry Christmas, indeed.

Tangled Lines

Help Tramp find the perfect present for Lady by picking the right path to the necklace.

1   2   3

Pretty Presents

Lady got a beautiful present for Christmas. Design your own Christmas presents here.

Odd Dog Out

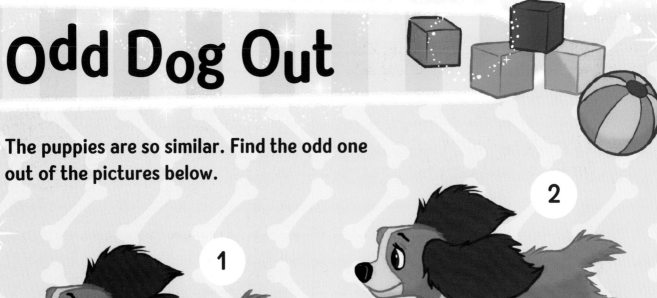

The puppies are so similar. Find the odd one out of the pictures below.

ANSWER: Picture 3 is odd one out.

Festive Find

Find all the Christmas words in this wordsearch.
Don't forget to look up, down and across.

c	a	r	o	l	p	x	d	o	g
j	e	c	w	u	r	s	k	y	i
t	b	f	r	i	e	n	d	s	w
i	v	a	c	a	s	w	i	n	c
n	o	m	s	x	e	d	r	o	v
s	w	i	r	p	n	x	k	w	u
e	n	l	m	u	t	r	e	e	l
l	x	y	f	q	s	c	z	p	s

carol　　　　**snow**
dog　　　　　**tinsel**
presents　　**tree**
friends　　　**family**

ANSWER:

69